S0-CSX-310

Antlers with Candles

PJ Publishing creates board books, picture books, chapter books, and graphic novels in multiple languages that represent the diversity of Jewish families today. By sharing Jewish narratives, values, and life events, we help families explore their connections with Jewish life.

All rights reserved. No part of this publication may be reproduced, distributed, or transmitted in any form or by any means, without the prior written permission of the publisher.

For information regarding permissions, please email permissions@hgf.org or contact us at:
PJ Library, a program of the Harold Grinspoon Foundation
67 Hunt Street, Suite 100
Agawam, MA 01001 USA

First published in 2015 by PJ Publishing, an imprint of the Harold Grinspoon Foundation
Reprinted in 2024
Text and illustration copyright © 2015 Harold Grinspoon Foundation
First Edition.
Designed by Massimo Mongiardo
1124/B0738/A3
ISBN 979-8-9891668-7-9
Printed in China
Manufactured for: Harold Grinspoon Foundation, 67 Hunt Street, Suite 100, Agawam, MA 01001

Antlers with Candles

written by Chris Barash
illustrated by Melissa Iwai

My toes were cold this morning
when I climbed out of bed.
I looked for my moose slippers...
I found other things instead.

What's that on the counter?

I tiptoe up to look.

It's just like the big antlers

on the moose in my new book!

I tried to see what's up there.
Uh-oh! I made it fall.
This looks like Daddy's cookie dough
but it's not sweet at all.

DREIDELS

Is that a bag of buttons?
What's in this sparkly box?
I see my favorite colors
on these funny, pointy blocks.

I hear my daddy coming.
Hooray! Hooray! Hooray!
Daddy sighs. “I need some coffee
before we talk. OK?

"This is our menorah.
It holds candles that will glow
and help us all remember
special times from long ago.

DREIDELS

"Mom made latkes." Daddy smiles
as he picks up the tray.
"The tasty pancakes warm us
on a cold and wintry day.

“Let’s pick up all these dreidels.
They’re fancy spinning tops.
We see a Hebrew letter
every time a dreidel drops.

“Tonight we’ll light the candles
with blessings and a song.
Soon you’ll have learned all the words
and you can sing along.

“We’ll smell onions and potatoes
as the crispy latkes fry.
We’ll eat Nana’s applesauce.
There’ll be sour cream to try.

"After dinner we'll play dreidel.
Your cousins will be here.
We'll use the buttons for our game
and whoever wins, we'll cheer!

"By then, you'll be so sleepy.
We'll hug and kiss goodnight.
But first, we'll have a party—
because Hanukkah starts tonight!"